GREEN LIZARDS
VS
RED RECTANGLES

Steve Antony

h
Hodder
Children's
Books

An imprint of Hachette
Children's Group

The **GREEN LIZARDS** and the **RED RECTANGLES** were at war.

The **GREEN LIZARDS** tried their best to defeat the **RED RECTANGLES,**

but the
RED RECTANGLES
were smart.

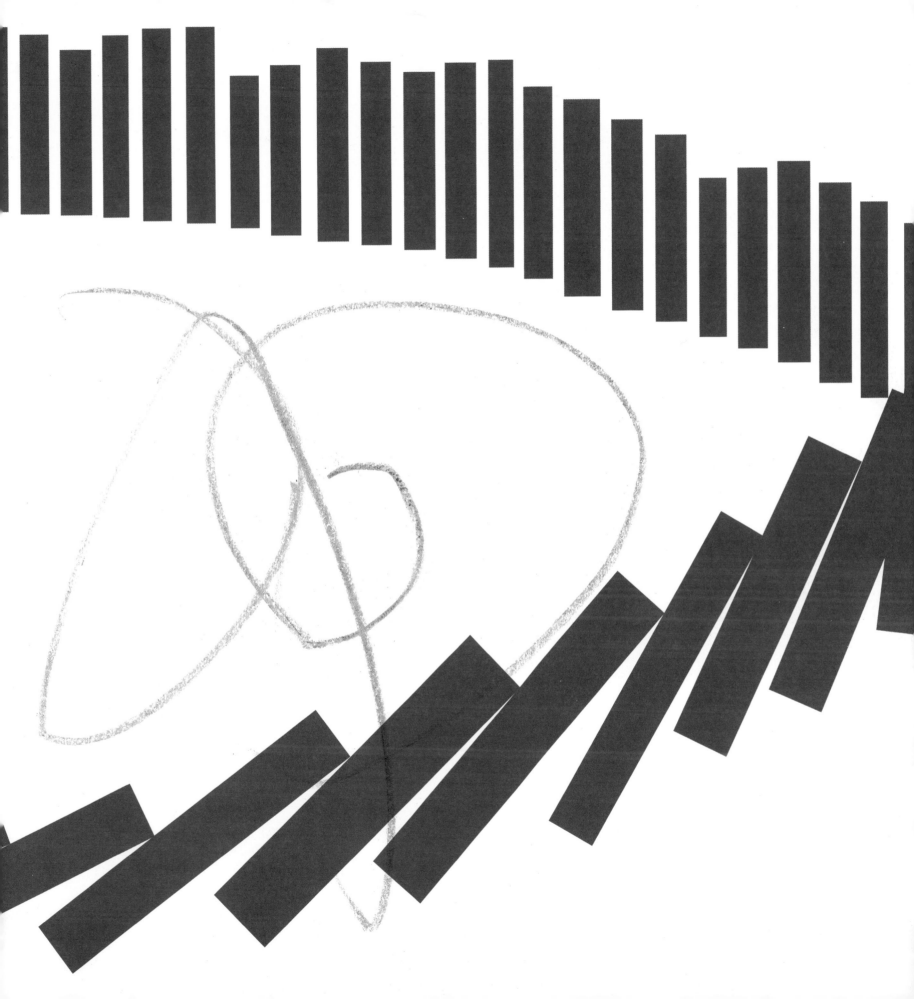

The **RED RECTANGLES** tried their best to defeat

the **GREEN LIZARDS,**

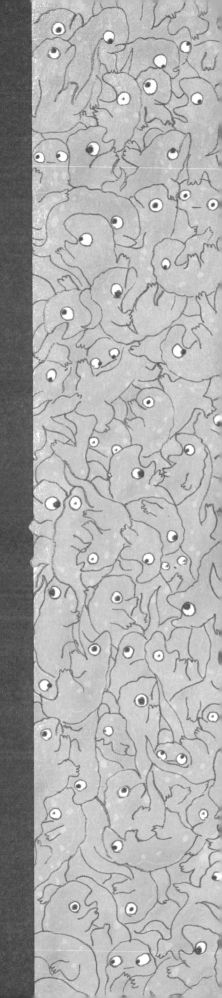

but the **GREEN LIZARDS** were strong.

WHAT ARE WE FIGHTING FOR?

asked one **GREEN LIZARD.**

But he was SQUASHED, and this led to...

THE BIGGEST WAR EVER. They fought...

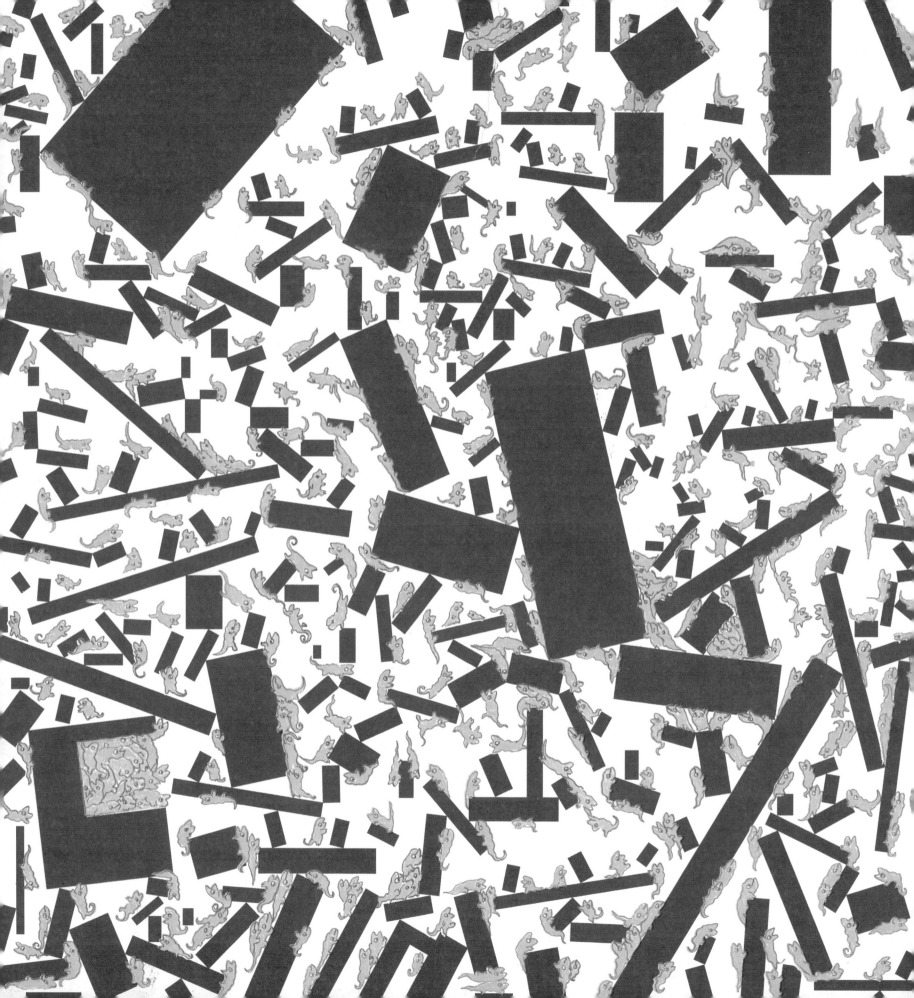

and fought and fought until...

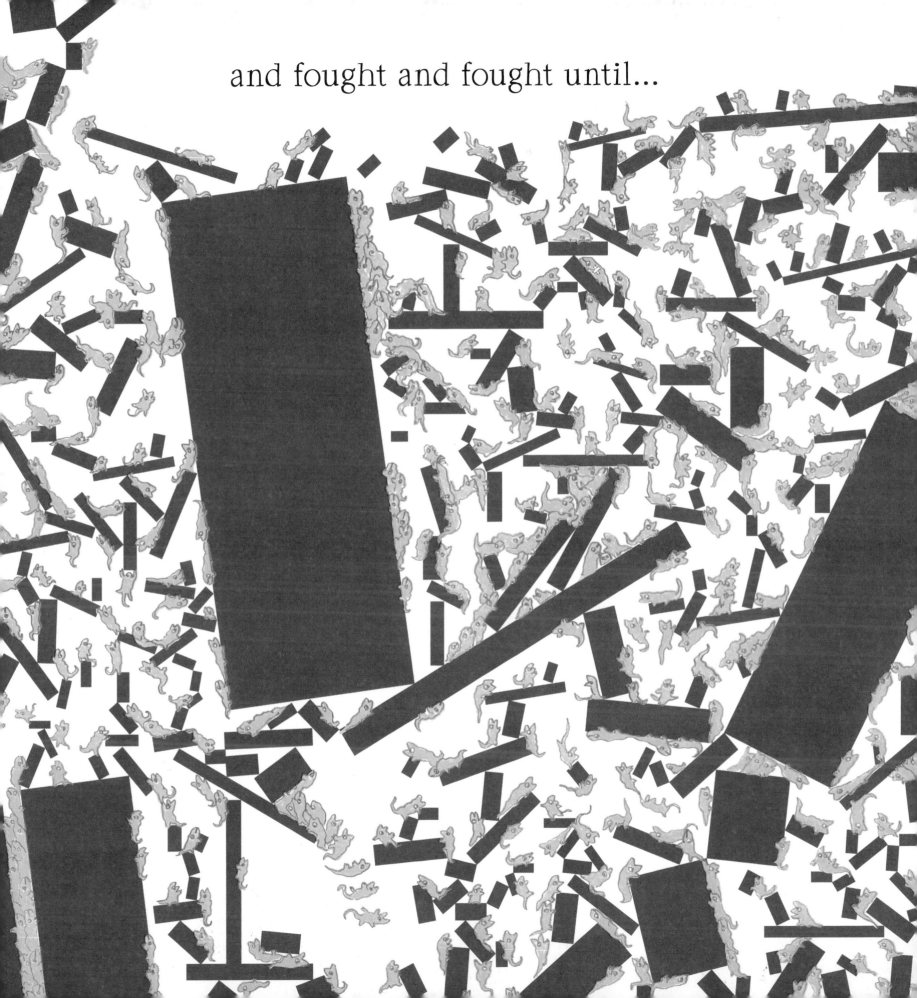

they could fight no more.

said one **RED RECTANGLE.**

The **GREEN LIZARDS** and the **RED RECTANGLES** gathered for a truce, and finally they found a way...

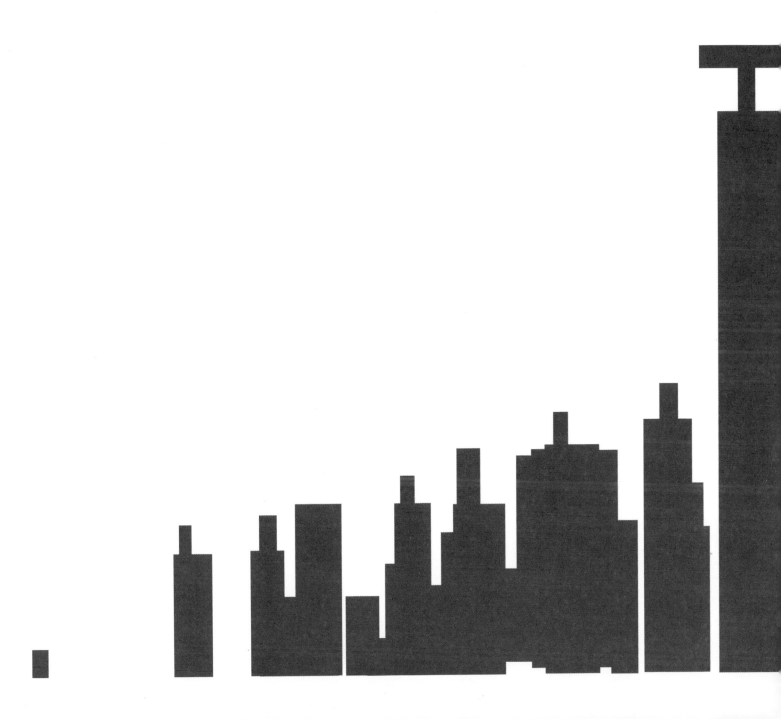

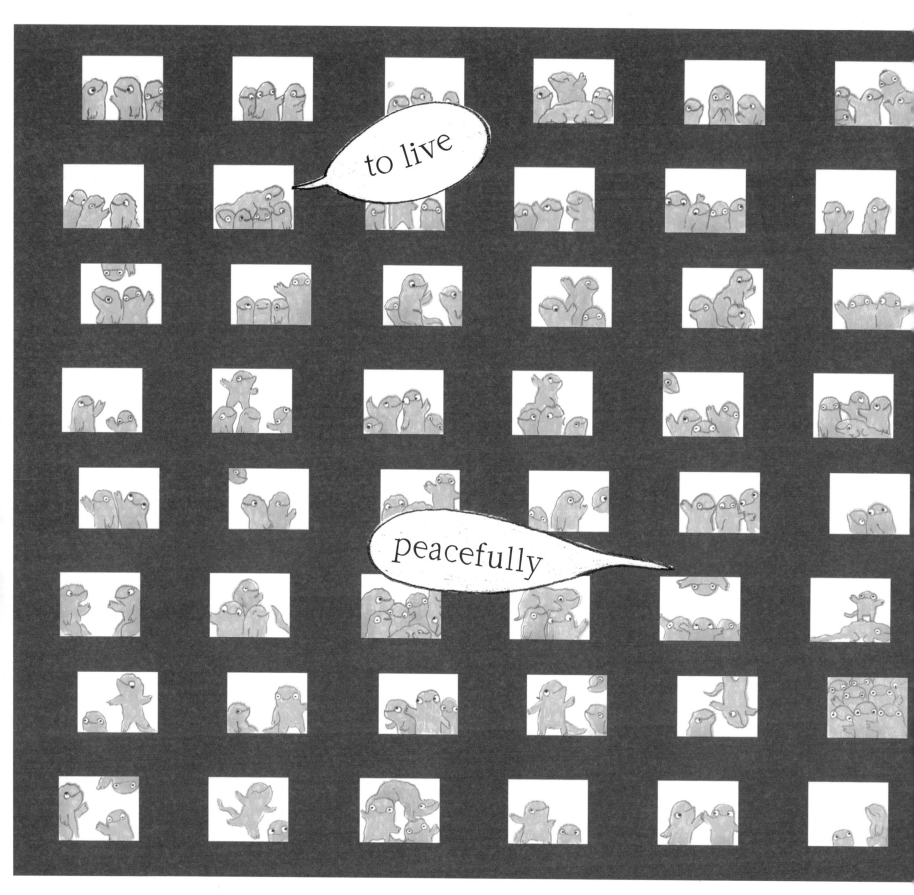

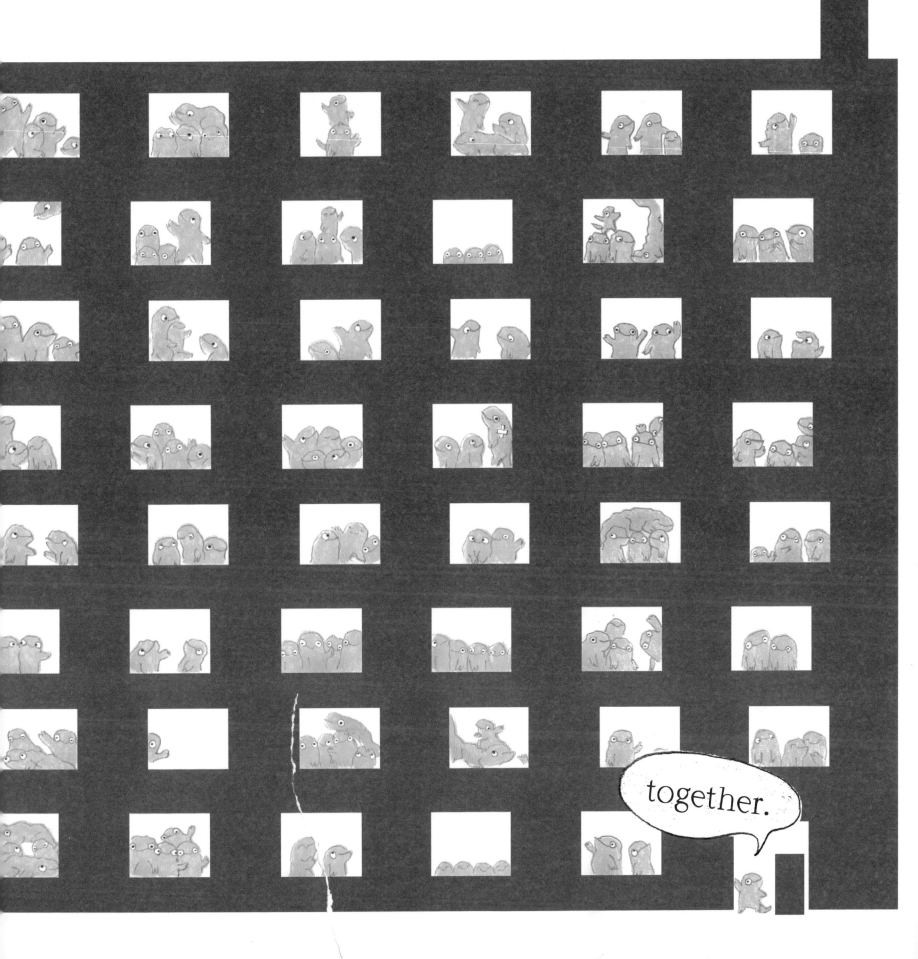